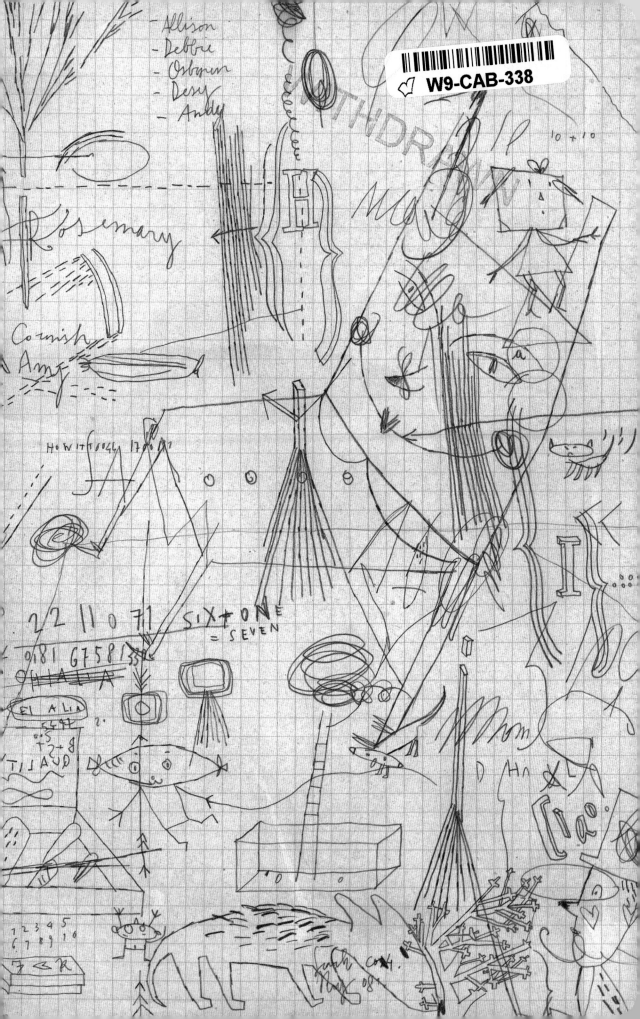

First U.S. edition 2000

Library of Congress Catalog
Card Number 99-75887

2 4 6 8 10 9 7 5 3 1

Printed in Hong Kong

This book was HANDLETTERED
by the author-illustrator.
THE ILLUSTRATIONS WERE DONE
IN COLLAGE.

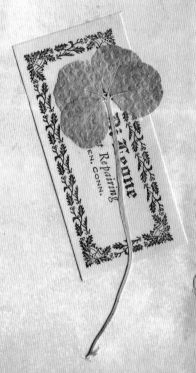

Candlewick
Press
2067
MASSACHUSETTS
Avenue
Cambridge,
MASSACHUSETTS
02140

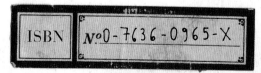
ISBN N⁰ 0-7636-0965-X

Sara Fanelli

Dear Diary

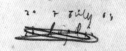

CANDLEWICK PRESS
CAMBRIDGE, MASSACHUSETTS

The habit of recording is first of all
likely to generate a desire to have
something of some interest to record;
it will exercise the memory and
sharpen the understanding generally;
and though the thoughts may not be
very profound, nor the remarks very
lively and ingenious, nor the narrative
of exceeding interest, still the exercise
is, I think, calculated to make the
writer wiser and perhaps better.

CHARLES C. F. GREVILLE
(from Diary, Jan 2, 1838)

per papà e
i nostri diari

Lucy's Diary

There was a little girl
who had a little curl
right in the middle of her forehead.
When she was good,
she was very, very good,
but when she was bad, she was horrid.
~ traditional

Lucy ♥

Dear Diary,
Today we each had to bring an insect to school to show the class. I wanted to bring Bulu, but Miss Star said a dog isn't an insect. I found a lovely LADYBUG in the garden and brought her along with me.

MY FR'ENDS LIKED HER A LOT, especially her BEAUTIFUL black spots!!

INSECT
• 3 PAIRS of LE
• 3 BODY SECTI
• WINGED

When Miss Star left the room for a minute, we started playing. A chair got thrown over by mistake.

me!

B.

oh, oh! sorry thair!

Miss Star was so ANGRY when she came back! She gave us a LOT of homework. We had to write the alphabet 10 times.

a A a A B B b C c C D
E e F F G G H h
I i I J j K K k L l
M m
Q q R R R S s T T t U u
V W w X x Y y Z Z

It took me all afternoon.

whoops! miss S. won't like this

ABC DE

It was getting late but I still took BUBU out to the park to pla

BUBU's friends

the POND

I hope BUBU is all right now. SHE seemed a bit UPSET today...

MY FRIEND AMY

MOM and DAD gave a party tonight and so we put out the nice Knives and forks. While we were eating, I saw a SHINY BRIGHT airplane in the sky.

It was flying really fast. No one else saw it because they were too busy admiring Bubu's good table manners.

GOOD old Bubu.

Star light Star bright FIRST Star I see tonight

CHAIR'S
DIARY

The place is very well
and quiet and the
children only scream
in a low voice.

LORD BYRON

DEAR DIARY,

IT WAS A LOVELY AND PEACEFUL MORNING UNTIL THE CHILDREN ARRIVED.

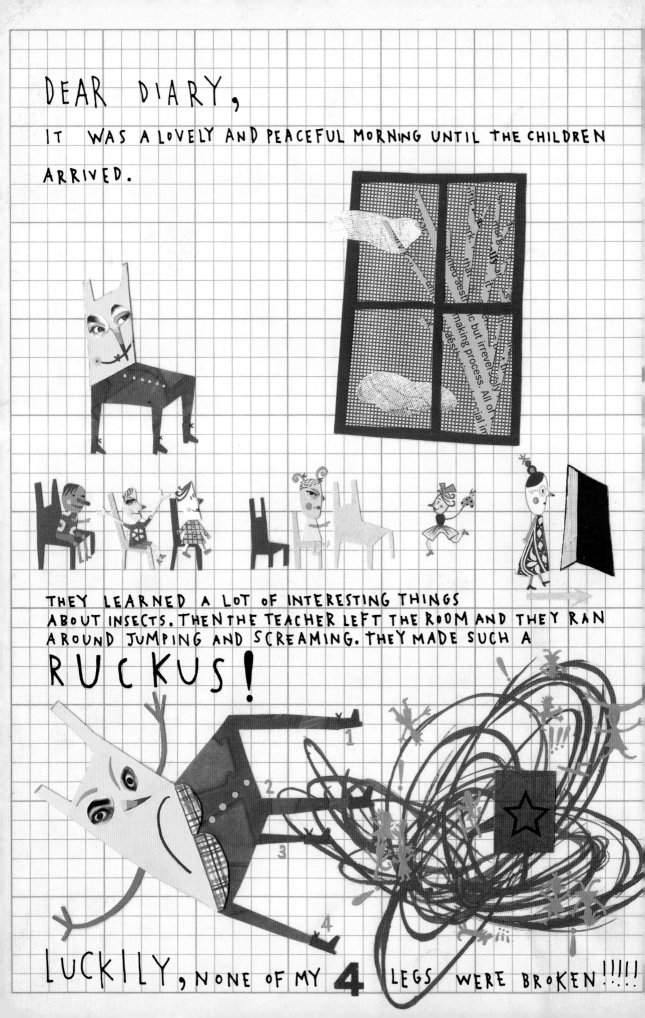

THEY LEARNED A LOT OF INTERESTING THINGS ABOUT INSECTS. THEN THE TEACHER LEFT THE ROOM AND THEY RAN AROUND JUMPING AND SCREAMING. THEY MADE SUCH A

RUCKUS!

LUCKILY, NONE OF MY 4 LEGS WERE BROKEN!!!!!

FROM THE FLOOR
THE CHILDREN SEEMED SO
DIFFERENT AND I NOTICED
SOMETHING VERY STRANGE ON
THE CEILING — A SPIDER
WITH WINGS!

AS SOON AS SCHOOL WAS OVER THE ROOM WAS NICE AND QUIET AGAIN.

Spider's Diary

"Will you walk into my parlor?"
said the spider to the fly:
"'Tis the prettiest little parlor
that ever you did spy."

MARY HOWITT

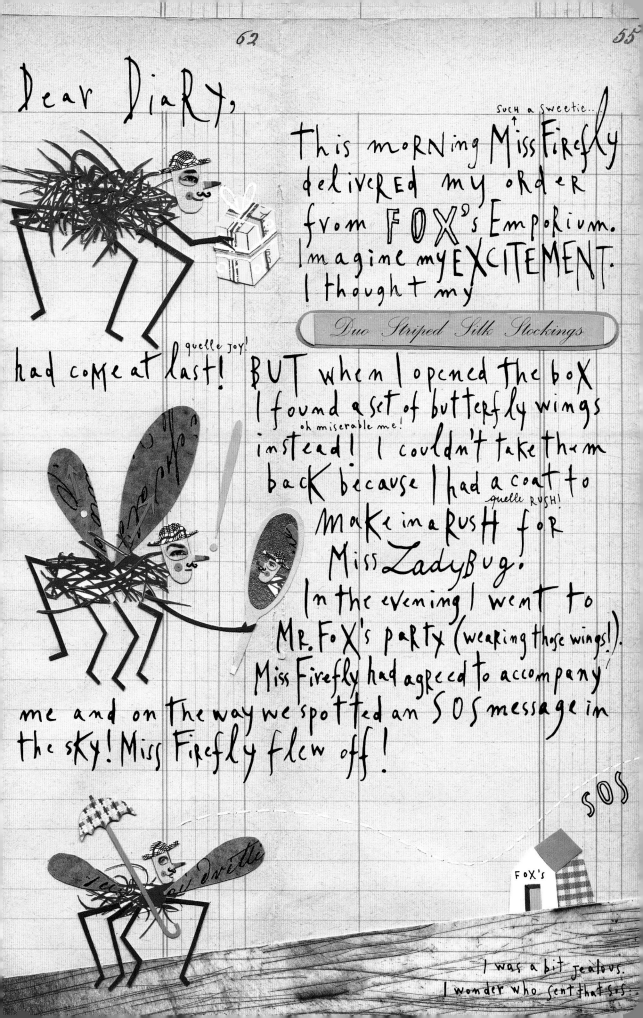

Dear Diary,

such a sweetie...

This morning Miss Firefly delivered my order from FOX's Emporium. Imagine my EXCITEMENT. I thought my

Duo Striped Silk Stockings

quelle joy!

had come at last! BUT when I opened the box I found a set of butterfly wings

oh miserable me!

instead! I couldn't take them back because I had a coat to

quelle RUSH!

make in a RUSH for Miss LadyBug!

In the evening I went to MR. FoX's party (wearing those wings!). Miss Firefly had agreed to accompany me and on the way we spotted an SOS message in the sky! Miss Firefly flew off!

SOS

FOX's

I was a bit jealous. I wonder who sent that SOS

The PARTY itself—well, what a SURPRISE!
All of my friends looked so ------------

DIFF

It turned out that FOX had switched all our orders on purpose. That Fox! He is always surprising us.

A wonderful party. AND Miss Firefly arrived in time to escort me home.

Firefly's Diary

Little lamps of the dusk,
You fly low and gold
When the summer evening
Starts to unfold.

CAROLYN HALL

Dear Diary,

Oh my, what a day! Hundreds of deliveries for Mr. Fox. Then I had to get ready for his party. I polished my light VERY BRIGHTLY.

On the way to the party with Mr. Spider I spotted an SOS in the sky and I flew after it. It came from a HUGE bird.

Knife and Fork's
Diary

It looked bad when the Duke of Fife
Left off using a knife,
But people began to talk
When he left off using a fork.

E. C. BENTLEY

K. + F.

Dear Diary,

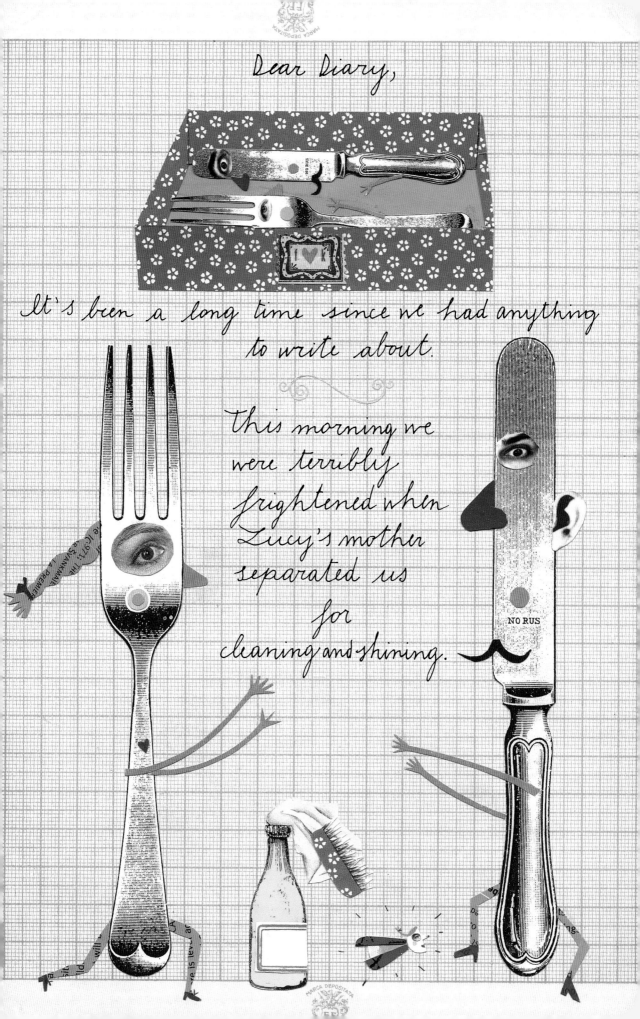

It's been a long time since we had anything to write about.

This morning we were terribly frightened when Lucy's mother separated us for cleaning and shining.

In the evening we met some old friends. The Plates are always so chatty and the Glasses so elegant. (We couldn't help remarking that none of the other knives and forks looked as well as we did!) But we had a scare when Mrs. Fork was accidentally dropped. To my relief, Bubu came to her rescue. Unfortunately Mrs. Fork felt the disgrace frightfully.

Now we hope to rest for a while in our cozy box.

BUBU'S
DIARY

 Dogs laugh, but they laugh with their tails. M. EASTMAN

DEAR DIARY,
SOMETIMES
IT'S HARD
TO BE
A
DOG.
↓

TODAY I THOUGHT
LUCY WAS GOING TO
TAKE ME ~~X~~ TO SCHOOL BUT
SHE TOOK A LADYBUG
INSTEAD. WOOF!
IN THE AFTERNOON I WAITED AND WAITED.
LUCY WROTE AND WROTE. BUT THEN ↑

WE PLAYED AND PLAYED IN THE PARK.

AT DINNER EVERYONE PATTED ME
AND GAVE ME CAKE. ALL
I DID WAS PICK UP MRS. FORK FROM
THE GROUND AND PUT HER ON THE TABLE.
I NEVER GET CAKE WHEN I PUT
MY BONES ON THE TABLE.
PEOPLE ARE VERY STRANGE.

Ladybug's
Diary

You are all fair, my love; there is no spot in you. SONG OF SOLOMON

Dear Diary,
This morning Lucy brought me to her school.
I was thrilled at first. I thought that the
class would
admire my
bright orange
coat. But when
everyone talked
just about my
spots, I became
very upset and flew away home as soon as I could.
At home all I could think about were those horrible
spots. I had to do something about them IMMEDIATELY.
Mrs. Ant and her family tried scrubbing them away
for me with strong soap but the spots remained.

BLACK
SPOTS!

SOAP

So then I asked Mr. Spider to make me a coat to wear over my spotted one and he kindly agreed even though he was a bit grumpy over some mix-up in the mail delivery today.

At Fox's party I met my friend Mr. GRASSHOPPER.
While we were dancing he confessed that he loved
me AND my black spots and asked me to MARRY HIM—
as long as I took the coat off forever !!!

EXCUSE me now, there is so
much to do for the
WEDDING ♡!